When I Miss You

WRITTEN BY Cornelia Maude Spelman

ILLUSTRATED BY Kathy Parkinson

Albert Whitman & Company
Morton Grove, Illinois

For R.—C.M.S.

To Gibson and Sterling, Ted and Elizabeth.
We will miss you!—K.N.P.

Books by Cornelia Maude Spelman
After Charlotte's Mom Died ~ Mama and Daddy Bear's Divorce
Your Body Belongs to You

The Way I Feel Books:
When I Care about Others ~ When I Feel Jealous
When I Feel Angry ~ When I Feel Sad
When I Feel Good about Myself ~ When I Feel Scared
When I Miss You

Library of Congress Cataloging-in-Publication Data

Spelman, Cornelia.
When I miss you / by Cornelia Maude Spelman ; illustrated by Kathy Parkinson.
p. cm. — (The way I feel)
Summary: A young guinea pig describes situations that make him miss his parents, how it feels to miss them,
and what he can do to feel better.
ISBN 0-8075-8910-1 (hardcover)
[1. Guinea pigs—Fiction. 2. Loneliness—Fiction. 3. Parent and child—Fiction.] I. Parkinson, Kathy, ill. II. Title. III. Series.
PZ7.S74727Wh 2004 [E]—dc22 2003014761

Text copyright © 2004 by Cornelia Maude Spelman. Illustrations copyright © 2004 by Kathy Parkinson.
Published in 2004 by Albert Whitman & Company, 6340 Oakton Street, Morton Grove, Illinois 60053-2723.
Published simultaneously in Canada by Fitzhenry & Whiteside, Markham, Ontario.
Printed in the United States.
10 9 8 7 6 5 4 3 2 1

The design is by Carol Gildar.

For more information about Albert Whitman & Company, please visit our web site at www.albertwhitman.com.
Please visit Cornelia at her web site: www.corneliaspelman.com.

Note to Parents and Teachers

Every parent and teacher knows that young children feel anxiety when separated from their mothers or fathers. And every parent and teacher must help children manage that anxiety, because separation is inevitable, either when a parent must work, or must be, for other reasons, absent for short periods of time.

How can we help? First, by not denying or minimizing children's anxiety. Separation causes genuine distress. Until children learn, by the repetition of separation and reunion, that a parent's return can be counted on, separation can feel like abandonment.

Young children's minds do not work like adults' minds. Children's sense of time is different. It is only with experience that children learn how to deal with separation.

To ensure that this learning takes place with a minimum of upset, we can do certain things:

Children's initial distress must be promptly and warmly attended to.

We need to leave children with a known caregiver, in a known setting—not with a stranger in a brand-new place.

We must provide children with their comforting objects.

Separations should not be longer than children of their age can tolerate. (Ask your pediatrician if you're not sure, or consult child development books.)

If we are not careful about these safeguards, separation can undermine children's development and sense of security. We want to be sure that children will be able, through repeated, successful experiences of separation, to say, "When I miss you, I know you'll be back!"

Cornelia Maude Spelman, L.C.S.W.

Sometimes I miss you.

I miss you when you have to go to work.

I want you, but you're not there.

When will you come back?

When you go out, I miss you.

I want to show you something, but I can't.
I wish you were with me!

I miss you if you have to take a little trip.

A few days seem like a long, *long* time.
I want you to kiss me goodnight.

I feel so happy when you come back!

Missing you is a heavy, achy feeling.

I don't like missing you. I want you right now!

But everybody misses someone sometimes.
We wish we could be together, but we can't.

Everyone has things they need to do.
Soon we'll see each other again.

When I miss you, there are ways others can help me.
They remind me that you'll be back.
They can snuggle with me or we can play.
It helps to be warm and close to someone.

There are ways I can help myself.
I can cuddle with my blanket
or stuffed animal.

I can get in a cozy
place and look at my
favorite book.

I can draw a picture
to show you.

When you go away, after a while I don't miss you as much.
I play and make things.

I laugh and have a good time.

Pretty soon you come back.

We're both glad to be together again!

When I miss you, I know you'll be back!